For A. J.
Have fun looking for falcons! I love you ♡
NANA

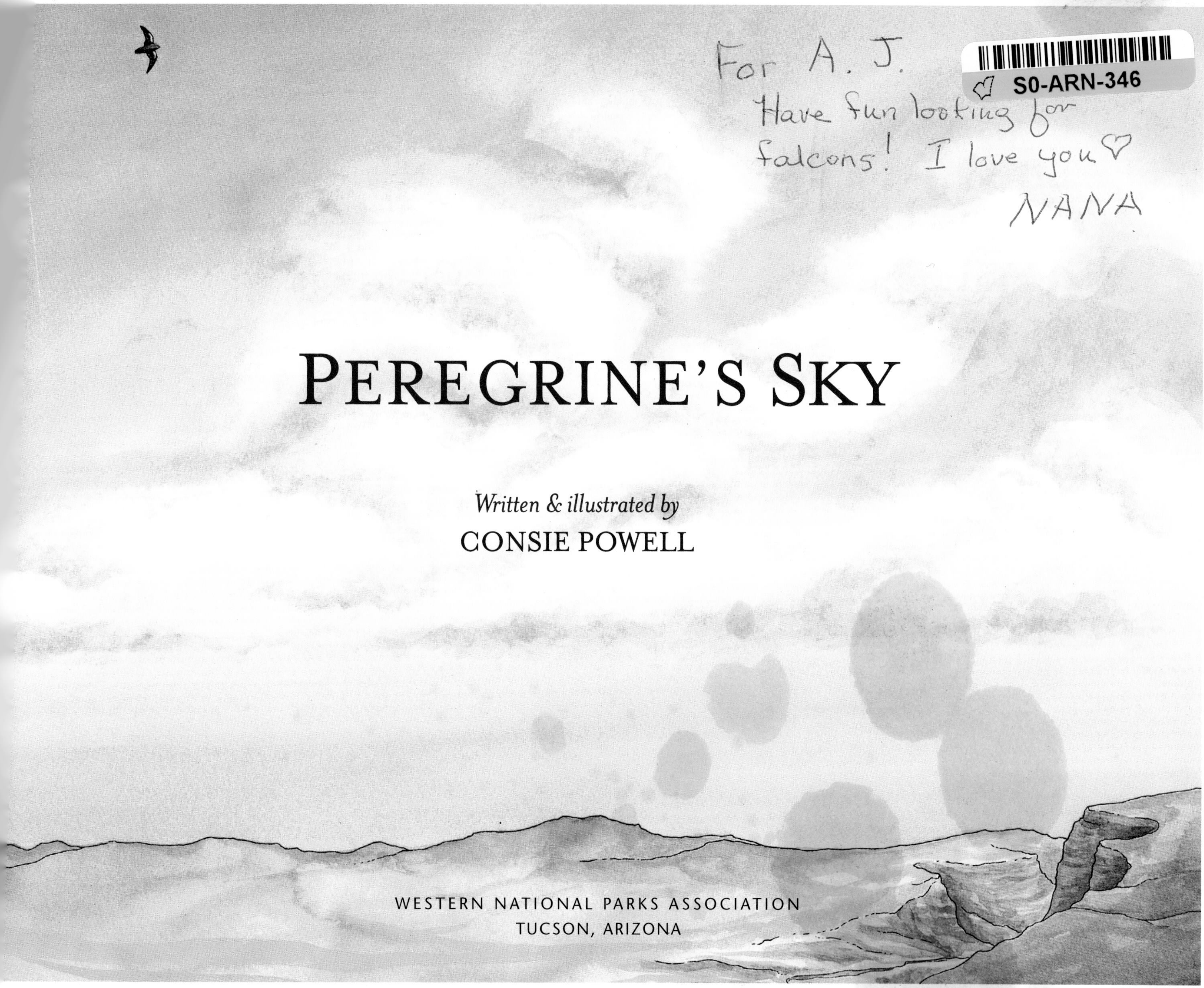

PEREGRINE'S SKY

Written & illustrated by

CONSIE POWELL

WESTERN NATIONAL PARKS ASSOCIATION
TUCSON, ARIZONA

High on a sheltered ledge, in a shallow scrape, rests one pale, speckled egg.

Before the egg, there were two falcons.
The male searched for a nest site:
a ledge on a steep cliff, safe and protected.
He poked and scratched to make a shallow basin.

Then he showed this nest to the female. He brought her gifts of food and danced with her in the sky, dipping and turning, chasing and courting. Now, high on a cliff they mate.

Peregrine falcons are crow-sized birds of prey, averaging 32 ounces for females and 22 ounces for males. They have sharp talons to capture prey and hooked beaks for tearing flesh. With long pointed wings and narrow tails, falcons are faster and more agile than any other predatory birds. Males (known as tiercels) are smaller than females (known as falcons). Pairs form enduring bonds; usually the same birds mate year after year. Frequently, they return to the same nest site.

A day after laying the first egg, the female produces a second. A day later, she lays a third egg. Then she spreads her warm feathers over the eggs and waits. The male brings food and feeds her. If she leaves the nest to hunt, the male broods the eggs to keep them warm. For days and weeks, the falcons brood and wait.

Peregrine falcons usually lay two to four eggs at intervals of 24 to 48 hours. The female does most of the incubating, turning the eggs and keeping them warm. This lasts for about 34 days.

A tiny hole appears in one egg. The hole becomes a crack. Finally, the shell falls away and a wet chick tumbles out. The mother inspects this tiny hatchling.

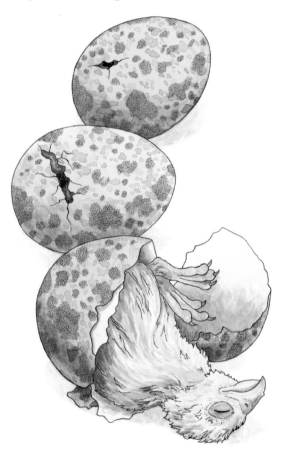

For their first two weeks, hatchlings depend on their parents for warmth, protection, and food. A falcon youngster still at the nest is called an "eyas."

Soon the chick is hungry. *"Skree! Skree! Skree!"* The father flies to the nest, a dead jay in his talons. The mother tears small scraps to feed to baby Peregrine. Two more days pass and two more eggs hatch. Now the scrape cradles three hungry and demanding chicks.

While their mother keeps the tiny chicks warm, their father brings food to his family. The babies grow fast and eat voraciously. By the time the chicks are two weeks old, both parents fly out to hunt. The parents flap and soar. They dive and loop. The male spies a dove, tucks his wings, and dives down to strike his prey in mid-air. The female flies up to meet him, somersaults, and grabs the meal from his talons. She rolls, spreads her wings, and carries the food to the ledge. The hungry youngsters scream in excitement, *"Skree! Skree! Skree! Skree! Skreeee!"*

s k r e

skree! skreeeee!

Peregrine falcons eat other birds such as ducks, shorebirds, and songbirds. They have exceptional eyesight and hunt by spotting prey from the air or a high perch. Researchers have clocked peregrine falcons diving at speeds as fast as 242 miles per hour—faster than most race cars! They overcome their prey in the air with swiftness and surprise.

The chicks continue to grow. After three weeks, dark feathers poke through the white down feathers. The two males are close in size. Peregrine is a female and already bigger than her brothers.

Around two weeks of age, flight feathers start to grow. By three weeks they are easily visible. The youngsters flap their wings to build strength, doing it ever more vigorously as they get older.

Soon, Peregrine and her brothers snoop beyond their nest scrape. They poke and prod, checking for leftovers. They wander the ledge and watch the sky, where their parents soar, dip, and dive. The chicks open their wings — flapping, reaching, exercising. They run and pump their wings.

Young wings grow stronger. Two flaps and a hop put Peregrine on a jutting boulder.

Three flaps propel her brother onto an outcrop. A bounce and a flap land him back on the ledge.

Hop, flap, jog, stretch. Three young falcons pump their wings and dance back and forth.

By 4 weeks old, the young falcons are close to adult weight. They start shedding their baby down and lose most of it within a week. Youngsters keep their brown juvenile plumage through their first year, molting to adult plumage when they are fully mature.

One morning, as Peregrine watches, one brother takes to the air. Their mother flies near, calling, encouraging. Soon he tires and flies to a tiny outcrop to land. He stumbles, then pushes himself back into the air. He flies toward his siblings and lands clumsily on the ledge.

Around 6 weeks old, the falcons take their first short flights. Males, are lighter and smaller, so they usually fledge first. It takes several weeks to master flying and landing.

The other brother leaves the ledge. He flaps, flies, and lands awkwardly. After a rest, both brothers take off again. Fly, then land. Their father flies close, calling, encouraging. Peregrine watches, beats her wings, and longs for the sky. But she is larger than her brothers, and heavier. She is not ready yet.

Kek Kek Kek!

As her brothers fly and practice landing, Peregrine paces and whips her wings. Her mother dips in front of her, calling, *"Kek kek kek!"* Her father soars before her, dangling food. For days, Peregrine screams and flaps, hops and stretches. She wants to fly!

Finally Peregrine pumps her wings and launches herself off the ledge. The sky is above her, below her, all around her.

She flies up and out.
She soars around
        and about.

She circles
        back,
    back,
back to her ledge.

Peregrine slows, skids only a bit, and lands.

Now the family lives in the sky, landing only to eat, preen, or rest. Peregrine sometimes flies alone, growing stronger with every wing beat. She flies with her brothers, chasing and playing tag. She grows more swift with every game. She tumbles with her father or chases her mother, growing agile and confident.

After fledging, the young falcons remain with their parents near the nesting area for a month or more. They practice their hunting skills, learning to feed themselves.

Peregrine can take any food that her flying parents pass to her as she flies. She can dive and grab it as it tumbles through the air. She can spot and chase prey that, so far, has always escaped. She is strong, agile, and fast. Now she wants to catch her own food.

High in the sparkling air, Peregrine soars. Her wings
glisten as she twists and turns. She notices everything:
the rippling stream, the cliffs to the west, her parents
perched and resting, her brothers flying.

Then she sees something else.

From a sandy spit, sandpipers rise. Peregrine tucks her wings and plummets — faster and faster — toward the flock. Eyes trained on one, she slices through the sky and strikes her prey dead. It tumbles through the air. Peregrine swoops behind and grabs it with her talons.

Peregrine's strong wings carry her to a ragged outcrop. Her sharp talons hold her prey as she eats. Her keen eyes gaze into the sky around her. She was born with a view of the sky. The sky will feed her, shelter her, and carry her far. For the rest of her life, this will always be Peregrine's sky.

ABOUT PEREGRINES

Peregrine, like young falcons all over the world, is ready for life on her own. She has learned to hunt, and no longer needs her parents. Now she will fly away and find her own wide open spaces with plenty of prey. When she is an adult, she will prefer high steep cliffs for nesting.

True to her scientific name, *Falco peregrinus* (the Latin word *peregrinus* means "wanderer"), Peregrine will probably travel far as she searches. As winter approaches, and prey becomes scarce, she may fly as far as Central or South America. She will need to be careful, too, for many young peregrine falcons do not survive their first year. They succumb to starvation or are killed by predators, poisons, or even by being shot during migration. As the seasons change, and the birds she feeds on fly north, Peregrine, too, will fly to where the food is most plentiful.

Had Peregrine been hatched in early China or Egypt, or in the middle ages in Europe, she might have been captured by a falconer and trained. She would have caught meat for her owner, and been loved and respected for this skill. But if she had lived when people started using guns for hunting and sport, Peregrine would have been considered an enemy and competitor, and might have been shot. This was the fate of many peregrine falcons and other birds of prey a hundred years ago.

But an even worse fate befell peregrine falcons in the 1940s and 1950s with the common use of DDT, a poison used to kill insects on crops. Poison seeped into plants and seeds, which were eaten by small birds. When large predatory birds such as peregrines ate these smaller birds the poisons passed into the falcons' bodies, where the toxins accumulated. The poison interfered with the manufacture of calcium, a mineral necessary for strong eggs. Peregrine egg shells were so thin that parents crushed the eggs with their bodies during incubation. Every year, fewer and fewer peregrine chicks hatched. North America and Europe banned DDT, but it was too late. In many areas, peregrine falcons were gone.

Bit by bit, conservation groups and dedicated individuals, with help and insights from contemporary falconers, worked to rebuild peregrine populations. Eggs were hatched in captivity. Young birds were returned to the wild and enough survived that some of them began to reproduce on their own. Now peregrine falcons live in wild and remote areas, as well as urban settings, where tall buildings substitute for steep cliffs.